AL RODIN

LITTLE
ECHO

Have you ever heard an Echo?

Maybe you have.
They live in lakes
and tunnels
and caves.

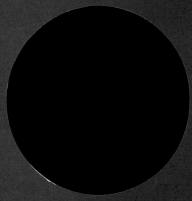

But have you
ever seen an Echo?

Little Echo was a very shy Echo.

She spent her days hiding
and sneaking
and searching
for sounds . . .

But whenever she heard the other beasts playing and laughing and making big **TAWOOs,** she longed to join in.

Yet all she could do was hide and echo from the shadows.

Nobody ever knew
she was there.

Then one day, Max arrived.

"I am here to find the **Treasure!**"

Max announced to the cave.

Treasure

Treasure

Treasure

Little Echo liked the sound of Treasure!
So she decided to **sneak** behind Max for a little while . . .

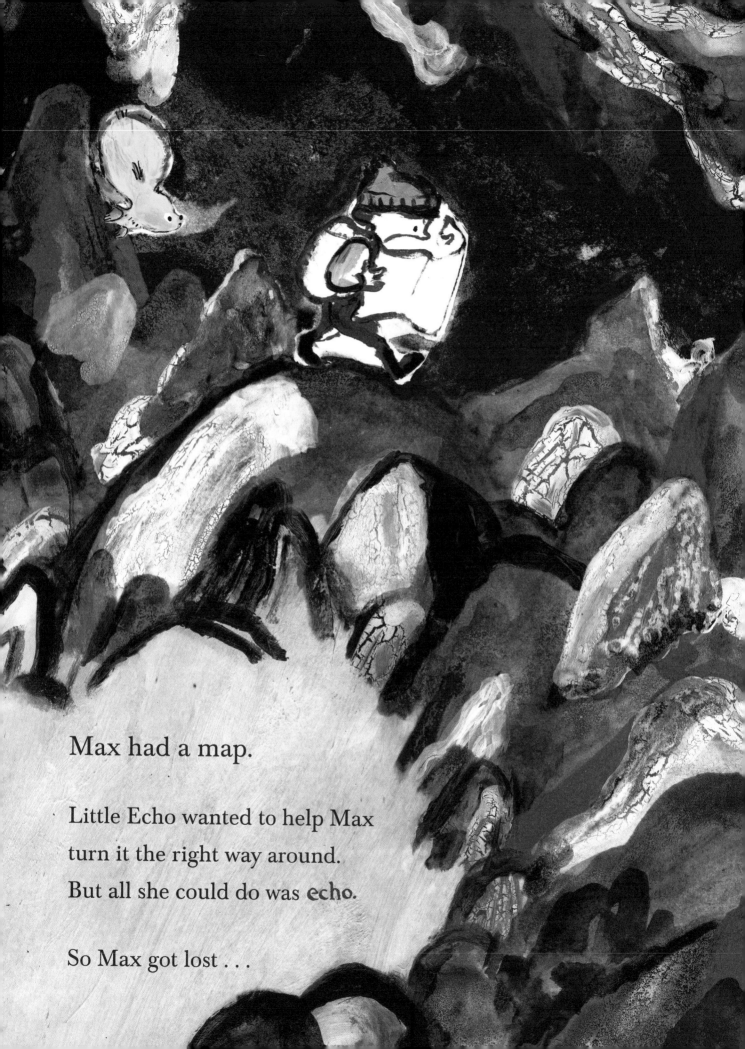

Max had a map.

Little Echo wanted to help Max
turn it the right way around.
But all she could do was echo.

So Max got lost . . .

Max had a spade.

Little Echo wanted to show Max
the best spots for digging.
But all she could do was echo.

So Max hit lots of rock . . .

Max had a plan!

"I will not leave this cave
until I find the Treasure!"
said Max.

Little Echo wanted to
tell Max that he was in
Bear's sleeping spot.

But she was too scared.
She couldn't even echo.

And then
        Bear came back . . .

And Bear was angry.

And Bear was hungry.

And Max was fast asleep.

So Little Echo gulped twice and pinched herself to be brave,
and for the first time in her life she got ready to say
her very own words . . .

"RUN!"

shouted Little Echo.

RUN!

RUN!

RUN!

UN!

UN

UN

UN

UN

UN

N

N

So Max ran.

And Little Echo ran too!

They hid until the coast was clear.
"You saved me!" said Max. "When I find
this Treasure, I'll give half of it to you!"

But Little Echo didn't want Max to leave
without her. She didn't want to go back
to the shadows.

So Little Echo gulped twice and pinched
herself to be brave, and for the second time
in her life she said her very own words . . .

"Could I look for the Treasure with you?" ou

ou

ou

said Little Echo. Her voice grew from a whisper.

"I have lots of ideas about where it might be." ee ee

ee

Max looked at Little Echo.

Little Echo looked at Max . . .

"All right," said Max.
"But I should warn you –
my map doesn't work."

Little Echo turned Max's
map the right way
around and off
they went.

As they searched, Max hummed.

As Max hummed, Little Echo echoed.

So Max echoed too . . .

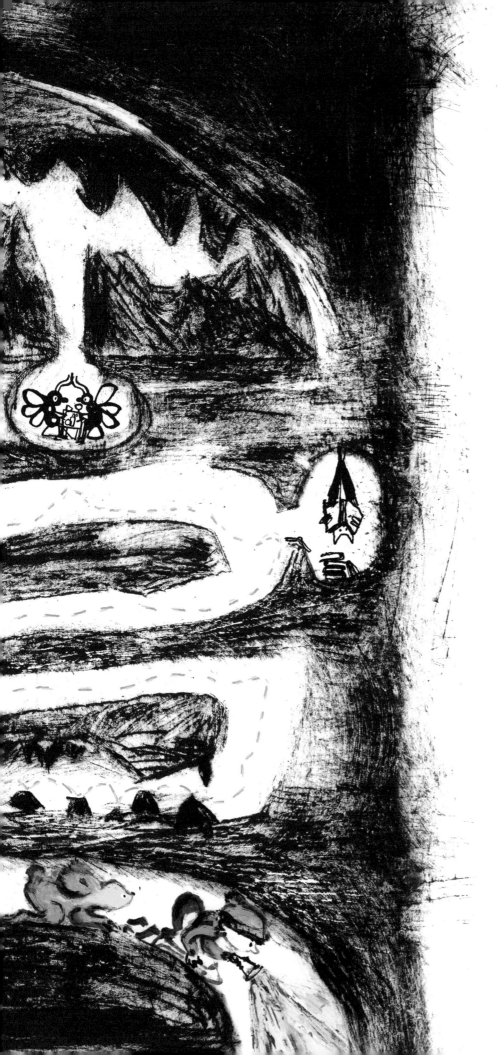

Together they
picked a spot
and drew a big

X.

And when they
were ready they

DUG

and

DUG

and

DUG.

Until
finally
they found . . .

...NOTHING.

"Maybe there really is no Treasure," said Little Echo.

This was a very disappointing thought.
A TERRIBLE and disappointing thought.

"Do you want to play something else?" said Max.
"How about **PIRATES?**" said Little Echo.
"I'll be the captain," said Max.
"And I'll be in charge!" said Little Echo.

So Little Echo and Max played pirates. They ate marshmallows. And stole a ship. And sailed off to smuggle things.

And Little Echo started to tell Max the secret things she had always wanted to say.

As Little Echo talked,
Max listened.
As Little Echo listened,
Max talked too.

And they were having such a good time listening and talking, and talking and listening that they forgot all about . . .

. . . the
Treasure.

For Kate

PUFFIN

PUFFIN BOOKS

UK | USA | Canada | Ireland | Australia | India | New Zealand | South Africa

Puffin Books is part of the Penguin Random House group of companies
whose addresses can be found at global.penguinrandomhouse.com.

Penguin
Random House
UK

First published 2021
001

Copyright © Al Rodin, 2021
The moral right of the author/illustrator has been asserted

Printed and bound in China
ISBN: 978–0–241–45087–1

The authorized representative in the EEA is Penguin Random House Ireland,
Morrison Chambers, 32 Nassau Street, Dublin D02 YH68

A CIP catalogue record for this book is available from the British Library

All correspondence to: Puffin Books, Penguin Random House Children's,
One Embassy Gardens, 8 Viaduct Gardens, London SW11 7BW